For Chris and Simone,
the best partners in crime.

EA

For Kel, who assures me, did NOT
make that smell. x

MB

Published in the UK by Scholastic, 2021
Euston House, 24 Eversholt Street, London, NW1 1DB
Scholastic Ireland, 89E Lagan Road, Dublin Industrial Estate, Glasnevin, Dublin, D11 HP5F

SCHOLASTIC and associated logos are trademarks and/or
registered trademarks of Scholastic Inc.

Text © Emma Adams, 2021
Illustrations © Mike Byrne, 2021

The right of Emma Adams and Mike Byrne to be identified as the author and illustrator of this work
has been asserted by them under the Copyright, Designs and Patents Act 1988.

ISBN 978 0702 30702 7

A CIP catalogue record for this book is available from the British Library.

Printed in Italy
Paper made from wood grown in sustainable forests and other controlled sources.

3 5 7 9 10 8 6 4 2

www.scholastic.co.uk

WHO MADE THAT SMELL?
SHH... DON'T TELL!

Emma Adams   Mike Byrne

SCHOLASTIC

In the kitchen this morning, I sat in my chair
and pointed my little nose into the air.
I gave a big frown as I had a good sniff,
and said to my dad,

"**Wowzers, what is that whiff?**"

Well, Dad went all rosy, his cheeks were quite red.
And I bet that you'll never guess just what he said . . .

There was a **big dinosaur**, that much is true –
she stopped by here earlier, needing the loo.
Her big, hefty footsteps rang out with a

BOOM!

as the stench of her **bottom burp**

filled up the room.

Although . . .

A **unicorn** might have arrived in a grump.

His tummy was aching – he needed to trump!

"**Woop!**"

He probably did it then let out a

Except . . . I can't see any **unicorn poop.**

But . . .

A **mermaid** was here – she had scales that were pink.

She turned on the taps and then sat in the sink,

and brushed out her hair with a comb made of shell.

Perhaps it was her who made this **awful** smell?

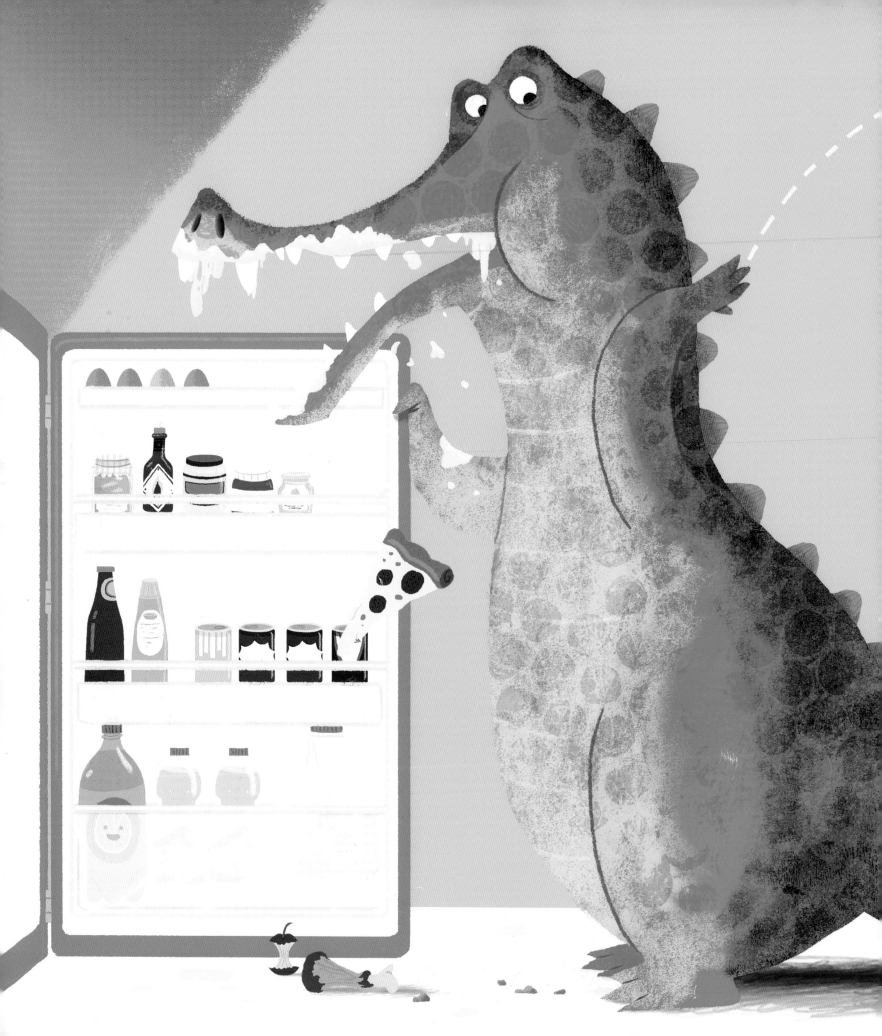

Of course, a **big crocodile** could have crawled through –
he clearly broke wind while he waited for you,
and must have searched through our small fridge for some food
then chomped it all down without asking –

how rude!

Also . . .

I *did* see a **skunk** - actually, it was cute!
That bundle of fur *clearly* let out a **toot!**
Then ran away quickly, that rascal, what cheek -
to come to our kitchen and make the place reek!

But . . .

TEETH

The **tooth fairy**, *they* might have been here – no doubt,
they were waiting for somebody's tooth to fall out,
then quite by mistake let a little one go.
Did magical dust come out? I'd like to know.

Or . . .

Maybe a **shark** splashed in here with a **flop**
and quite accidentally let out a small pop!
Fins? Very wiggly. Tail? Oh-so-long.
But would a shark parp really make such a **pong?**

But what if a **dragon** swept in super-fast,
and let out a terribly loud bottom **blast?**
Then quietly sat down right here with a plonk –
I'm telling you, that dragon made *such* a honk.

My dad looked at me after talking a while,
then chuckled a little and gave me a smile.

I thought very carefully – *could* it be true?
And if not those creatures, then, who did it? WHO?!

**Well, thinking about it, a smell quite *that* bad
could really have only been made by . . .**

. . . my dad!

"Ha!" my dad laughed. "Yes, that was MY show-stopper – my **talented bottom** created that **whopper!**"

So it *wasn't* a unicorn who did the crime,

no shark and no dragon – at least . . .

. . . *not* this time!

Unicorn Hoops

CHOCO